Too Many K

Written by Roger Befeler
Illustrated by Rose Mary Berlin

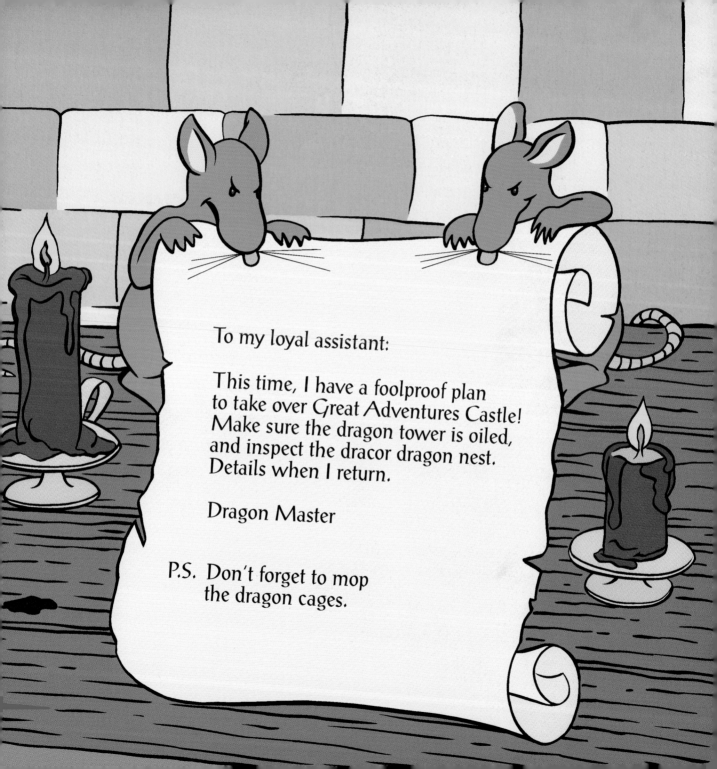

One misty morning at Great Adventures Castle, a knight on guard duty saw an unusual object out beyond the moat. As he came closer, he realized the object was an enormous spotted egg.

"Hmm. This huge egg will get in the way of our jousting matches. I'd better take it inside," the knight said. It took three knights and a horse to carry the egg into the castle.

The royal chef was about to make breakfast when he saw the gigantic egg. "You know, with this egg I can make an omelet big enough for King McBeard and all his court," he said to himself.

He put his shoulder against the egg and pushed as hard as he could. The egg rolled into the kitchen and came to rest near the fire. The chef then turned to the larder to gather ingredients for the mammoth omelet.

As the fire began to warm the egg, it started shaking. The egg tossed and turned. Then it cracked. The amazed chef watched as ten baby dragons hatched from the huge egg.

"*Squarble! Squarble!*" the dragons chirped.

"Oh my," said the chef to the dragons. "No giant omelet for the king *this* morning. I'd better round you up before His Royal Highness sees you. Everyone knows King McBeard likes his mornings quiet."

The baby dragons started hopping about the kitchen.
They were very curious and very, very hungry.
Two of the dragons gobbled up a freshly baked sponge cake.
Others dived into a barrel of apples, knocking it over and
scattering apples across the floor.
"Wait! Stop that!" the chef cried in dismay.

Suddenly, the kitchen door flew open. It was King McBeard! Apples and baby dragons nearly knocked him over.

"What, pray tell, is going on here?" asked the king.

"Oh, Sire, a thousand humble apologies. These dragons are wrecking my kitchen! They'll destroy the castle next!"

King McBeard took charge, as kings like to do.
"Bring me the yellow pages," the king roared.
Two pages dressed all in yellow appeared.
"Find a dragon catcher," he commanded. Faster than
you can say *squarble,* the yellow pages returned
with a dragon catcher.

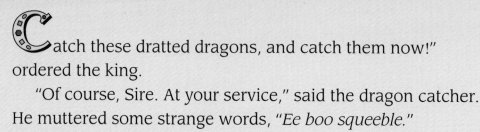

"atch these dratted dragons, and catch them now!" ordered the king.

"Of course, Sire. At your service," said the dragon catcher. He muttered some strange words, *"Ee boo squeeble."*

Four of the dragons perked up their ears and quickly made a circle around the king.

"Impressive," said the king. As he tried to step forward, the dragons sat on his feet and leaned against him. The king couldn't move! The king's knights looked on helplessly.

It seems you have a more serious problem than you thought," laughed the dragon catcher.

Holding out a claw-like hand, he added, "Let me introduce myself. I *am* a dragon catcher. I used my dragons to catch you! But you know me as someone else."

I should have suspected it was you, Dragon Master!" said King McBeard.
"That's right," said the dragon master. "Either you hand over your crown, or I'll have my dragons do more than keep you from moving."
The dragons smiled, chirped, and nuzzled the king's feet.

"Give up my crown? Never!" cried King McBeard.

The dragon master replied, "You'll soon have no choice. These are baby dracor dragons. In two days they will grow to three times the size of a knight."

Just then, a rumbling sound could be heard outside.

"Ah," said the dragon master. "That must be my loyal assistant with the dragon tower. McBeard, your reign is over."

The tower, which looked like a dracor dragon, rolled up to the window. All the knights trembled as they heard the call of a mighty dragon echo from the castle walls.

But the baby dragons did not tremble. They were excited—and delighted.

"Squarble! Squarble!" the dragons chirped. One by one, they hopped out the window and onto the head of the dragon tower.

Wait!" cried the dragon master frantically. "*Corkee noo noo squarble!*" But his words were drowned out by chirps.

The weight of the baby dragons carried the tower away from the castle. Abandoned by his army of baby dragons, the dragon master was powerless.

Without wasting a second, the knights seized the dragon master.
For his misdeeds, King McBeard banished him from the castle forever.
"That was close," said the king. "Luckily, he brought one too many dragons!"